This book belongs to

_____

For my godchild, Robert
D.A.

For Todd Christopher Chamberlain
D.S.S.

EASTER TREASURES
Favorite Stories and Poems for the Season

COMPILED AND EDITED BY DIANE ARICO
ILLUSTRATED BY DANIEL SAN SOUCI

Doubleday
NEW YORK LONDON TORONTO SYDNEY AUCKLAND

Acknowledgments

The Easter Bunny That Overslept by Priscilla and Otto Friedrich, text copyright © 1957 by Otto Friedrich. Reprinted by permission of Lothrop, Lee & Shepard Books.

"The Rabbits' Song Outside the Tavern," reprinted with permission of Macmillan Publishing Company from *Away Goes Sally* by Elizabeth Coatsworth. Copyright 1934 by Macmillan Publishing Company, renewed 1962 by Elizabeth Coatsworth Beston.

Easter Fires adapted by permission of Wilma Pitchford Hays from the story published by Coward-McCann, copyright © 1959 by Wilma Pitchford Hays.

"Easter Morning" from *Rabbits, Rabbits* by Aileen L. Fisher, copyright © 1983 by Aileen L. Fisher. Reprinted by permission of Harper & Row Publishers, Inc.

"Meeting the Easter Bunny" from *Songs from Around a Toadstool Table* by Rowena Bastin Bennett. Copyright © 1967 by Rowena Bastin Bennett. Reprinted by permission of Modern Curriculum Press, Inc.

Easter Bunny's Breakfast by Miriam Clark Potter, reprinted with permission by Constance P. Bruce.

"Baby Seed Song" by Edith Nesbit, reprinted by permission of John Farquharson, Ltd., London.

Published by Doubleday, a division of Bantam Doubleday Dell Publishing Group, Inc., 666 Fifth Avenue, New York, New York 10103.

Doubleday and the portrayal of an anchor with a dolphin are trademarks of Doubleday, a division of Bantam Doubleday Dell Publishing Group, Inc.

Library of Congress Cataloging-in-Publication Data
Easter treasures: favorite stories and poems for the season /
compiled and edited by Diane Arico; illustrations by Daniel San Souci.
p. cm.
Summary: Presents a collection of stories and poems expressing
Easter and springtime themes, including "The Velveteen Rabbit," "The
Selfish Giant," "The Easter Bunny That Overslept," and poetry by
such authors as Elizabeth Coatsworth and Aileen Fisher.
1. Easter—Literary collections.   2. Spring—Literary collections.
3. Children's literature, American.   4. Children's literature,
English.   [1. Easter—Literary collections.   2. Spring—Literary
collections.   3. American literature—Collections.   4. English
literature—Collections.]   I. Arico, Diane.   II. San Souci, Daniel, ill.
PZ5.E28   1989
810'.8'033—dc19   87-362426

ISBN 0-385-24401-0

ISBN 0-385-24402-9 (lib. bdg.)

Contents

The Easter Bunny That Overslept

Priscilla and Otto Friedrich

In his cozy warm burrow under the ground, the Easter Bunny was sound asleep. He was dreaming of Easter and the brightly painted eggs that he was going to bring to all the children. Easter came at last, but the Easter Bunny kept right on sleeping. There was no sun to wake him up, and it rained all day long. The children were very disappointed not to find any eggs hidden on their lawns, or in their homes. But their parents had bought some jelly beans so they weren't completely forgotten. It rained every day for a month—and the Easter Bunny slept right on!

Early in May the rain stopped. The sun shone into the Easter Bunny's burrow and woke him up. He yawned and stretched, and put on his new clothes because, of course, he thought it was Easter time. He even sang a little song to himself—

I hip and I hop A pink one for you,
My eggs are blue, All nice and new.
Red, and green too. Hippety-hop!

Soon he came to a pink house where a mother and a father, a girl and a boy, and a baby were sitting under an apple tree.

They were eating chocolates—all except the baby. He was too little for chocolates, so he held a cracker.

The Easter Bunny hopped up and started singing "Happy Easter to You." It had the same tune as "Happy Birthday."

When the Easter Bunny finished his song, he offered his basket of Easter eggs.

"What's all this?" asked the father. "What is this rabbit doing here?"

"Why, it's the Easter Bunny," said the little girl.

"But Easter was weeks ago!" said the mother. "Today is Mother's Day."

"Bye-bye!" said the baby. These were the only words he could say, so he said them over and over. The Easter Bunny decided to try somewhere else. He looked sadly back as he hopped to a yellow house nearby. But no one there wanted any Easter eggs either. He hopped all through the neighborhood, but everywhere he heard the same thing. It was too late for Easter eggs. Some of the people even scolded him for not being on time.

The Easter bunny went back to his burrow. He looked at his beautiful basket of Easter eggs that nobody wanted. He thought and he thought. Finally he had an idea. "I'll be a Fourth-of-July Bunny!" he said to himself. And he started repainting his eggs red, white and blue. Then he made himself a red, white and blue hat. And on the Fourth of July, he started out again.

It was a very hot day, and the bunny's basket began to feel heavier and heavier as he hopped along. When he came to the center of the town, he saw a crowd of people watching a parade.

The band came first, with trumpets and trombones going

7

"Ooom-pah-pah." Then came soldiers, then came the Boy Scouts and the Girl Scouts carrying flags.

And with them, proudly carrying his basket full of red, white and blue eggs, hopped the Fourth-of-July Bunny.

"Stop the parade!" shouted an officer. "Stop! Halt!"

Everyone stopped.

"What's all this?" the officer demanded. "Who are you?"

"Well, I'm really the Easter Bunny," the rabbit said in a very small voice. He was beginning to be a bit frightened. "But I overslept a little and started out too late and nobody wanted my Easter eggs. So I thought I'd be a Fourth-of-July Bunny."

"The Fourth-of-July is no time for *eggs!*" The officer looked very cross. "Now go away!"

Just then a great firecracker went BOOM! The children all clapped their hands in delight at the noise. None of them paid any attention to the Easter Bunny.

Bang! Bang! Bang! Smaller firecrackers were going off now. Then a cluster of great rockets went zooming into the sky and turned into a cluster of stars.

The parade marched on, and the Easter Bunny was left alone.

He tried knocking at several more doors, but everyone thought he was joking. So he went back to his burrow and fell asleep again. The summer passed and the days grew shorter. The leaves blew down from the trees, and still the Easter Bunny slept.

One black night when the wind howled outside, the Easter Bunny heard a loud knock. He jumped up and opened his door. Three little white ghosts stood in front of him. "BOO!"

Just then the wind blew very hard. The white sheets flapped on the three little ghosts. The Easter Bunny looked down and saw three pairs of brown shoes.

It was Halloween.

"A trick or a treat!" one of the ghosts cried.

"Wait right there," the Easter Bunny said happily, and he went back into his den to get his Easter eggs.

"A trick or a treat!" the children repeated as he returned with his basket. When they saw the red, white and blue eggs, the tallest child said, "What is this?"

"They're Fourth-of-July eggs," said the Easter Bunny.

"But this is Halloween!" said the middle-sized child.

"Well, they're really Easter eggs," the unhappy bunny explained. But he was too tired to tell his whole story all over again because he already knew that nobody wanted his eggs.

"Easter eggs on Halloween," the smallest child said. "That's no treat."

The Easter Bunny hung his head. He looked so sad that the children didn't even play a trick on him. They just ran away laughing.

"Easter eggs on Halloween!" they shouted, their voices getting farther and farther away. "Easter eggs on Halloween! Whoever heard of such a thing!"

The Easter Bunny stood in his doorway and watched them go.

9

He began to shiver. The wind was cold and blowing harder. He waited and waited for some more children to come. It started to snow. Suddenly, a fierce gale swept the little rabbit off his feet and carried him high up in the air.

When at last he came down, he blinked and rubbed his eyes. At first all he could see was snow. Then he caught sight of a sign that said SANTA'S HOUSE. The sign was shaped like an arrow and it was pointing to a curving path that led between two rows of Christmas trees.

The Easter Bunny hopped down the path and there, just around the bend, he saw the house. The next moment he was knocking timidly on the door.

Santa himself opened it. "Well, bless my soul!" he said when he saw the bunny on his doorstep. "Come in! Come in!"

So the Easter Bunny went in, and once more he told his story —how he had overslept, how nobody wanted his eggs, how he tried to be a Fourth-of-July Bunny, how he had been chased away, how the children had come to his burrow to frighten him on Halloween.

"Well, well," said Santa Claus. "Well, well, well! There's nothing we can do about your Easter eggs, of course. But if you want to help make the children happy, I have plenty of work for you to do." And almost before he knew it, the Easter Bunny was busy painting toy fire engines, and tops, and doll beds and many more toys. He was having such a good time, he forgot all about the Easter eggs that nobody wanted.

On Christmas Eve, Santa loaded the toys on his reindeer sleigh, and when he was ready to start he said to the bunny, "That's the biggest load I ever had. Maybe you'd better come along and help me tonight." So the Easter Bunny hopped in the sleigh next to Santa and off they flew through the sky.

Sometimes Santa would say the chimney was a little too narrow for him to climb down.

Then the Easter Bunny would take some toys from Santa's pack, slide easily down the narrow chimney, and put the toys in the children's stockings that were hanging by the fireplace.

And Santa Claus would say, "I never could go up and down all those chimneys as fast as that!"

And they would ride gaily on to the next house.

But after they had delivered the last present, the Easter Bunny began to feel a little tired from all his traveling. He decided to go back to his burrow and sleep until Easter came again.

"Wait a minute," Santa Claus said. "I have a Christmas present for you, too." He reached deep into his sack and brought out a beautiful gold alarm clock.

"Oh, thank you, thank you, Santa Claus. I'll set it to go off Easter Sunday."

And the next year when the gold alarm clock began to ring, the Easter Bunny jumped up and filled *two* baskets full of eggs. Then he hopped up to the same pink house that he had visited the year before. A little boy called "Hi, Easter Bunny." It was the same baby who could only say "Bye-bye" the year before.

"Happy Easter!" the Easter Bunny called gaily. He offered the little boy an Easter egg, and the little boy took it.

The Easter Bunny was very happy. It was so nice to be right on time. And because of his gold alarm clock, he was never late delivering his Easter eggs again.

The Rabbits' Song Outside The Tavern

Elizabeth Coatsworth

We, who play under the pines,
We, who dance in the snow
That shines blue in the light of the moon,
Sometimes halt as we go—
Stand with our ears erect,
Our noses testing the air,
To gaze at the golden world
Behind the windows there.

Suns they have in a cave,
Stars, each on a tall white stem,
And the thought of a fox or an owl
Seems never to trouble them.
They laugh and eat and are warm,
Their food is ready at hand,
While hungry out in the cold
We little rabbits stand.

But they never dance as we dance!
They haven't the speed nor the grace.
We scorn both the dog and the cat
Who lie by their fireplace.
We scorn them licking their paws
Their eyes on an upraised spoon—
We who dance hungry and wild
Under a winter's moon.

Easter Fires

Adapted from the story by
Wilma Pitchford Hays

It had been many months since Little Bow's village had seen rain. Night and day, the people danced before the council fires and prayed to the Great Spirit to send rain. But no rain had come.

Now, as Little Bow sat beside the dry bed of sand where a cool stream had run before the drought, he heard the drumbeats sounding.

"E-ya, Star-in-the-Face," he said to his pretty black pony with the white mark on her forehead. "The drumbeats are calling a council meeting. I must go."

Little Bow left his pony under a cedar tree and hurried to the gathering.

There he looked around at the solemn faces gathered before the council ring. He looked at the face of his father, Big Bow, and at Chief Hah-nee. He saw the bowed head of Matawanee, the blue-bead maker, and Katakomo, the medicine man. Katakomo was a big, heavy man, whose power was great in times of deep trouble. Now he rose to speak.

"My people," he began, "you have shown bravery in times of great danger. But now bravery is not enough. Even the animals we must have for food have gone away because there is no water. Only strong medicine can save our tribe now.

"I have fasted and made many prayers," the medicine man continued. "I have called upon the Fire Gods to give us a sign. What will please them? What will turn away their anger and cause them to send life-giving rain?

"The Great Spirit will answer. We must sing the song of fire and rain. We must watch for his sign."

"E-ya," the people answered.

They began to sway back and forth to the drum sounds. Their voices rose in prayer songs. Young braves danced about the fire, drawing nearer and nearer to its heat, which was no more scorching than the sun overhead. Little Bow grew excited as he sang with his people, "E-ya, give us a sign, God of fire and rain."

The day moved into afternoon and the sun blazed down. The voices of the people grew hoarse. Some braves fell forward upon the ground.

Little Bow tried to keep praying but his thoughts wandered. If only Silver Arrow were here. Silver Arrow was the sweetest singer among all the young braves and his dancing was most graceful. The Great Spirit would listen to him and give a sign. But Silver Arrow had gone to guide the white missionary padres to the mountaintop where they would build their mission.

Little Bow was proud that his sister, White Fawn, was to be married to Silver Arrow when he returned. But this would only happen if the Great Spirit heard their prayers and sent rain, and the people lived.

The approach of White Fawn interrupted the boy's thoughts. He saw his sister come from their lodge with a flat corn cake in her hand. She moved among the people toward their father and knelt beside him.

"Father, I bring you a cake to give you strength to sing again," White Fawn said softly.

Big Bow took the cake but dropped his head again. "Please eat, my father," White Fawn said. "You must grow strong and sing prayers again. The God of Fire must send a sign or we shall all die."

The man bit into the cake and White Fawn smiled. She rose to leave. As she passed the council fire, her doeskin skirt fanned the coals and the flames leaped high. Katakomo, the medicine man, jumped to his feet.

"The sign," he cried hoarsely. "You saw the flame leap high. White Fawn must be offered to the God of Fire. White Fawn must die."

Little Bow thought he must be imagining Katakomo's words. But when he heard the women and children begin to wail and saw the dancers standing still as if turned to stone, he knew Katakomo's words were real.

"It has been many years since the Great Spirit asked a life from us," Katakomo said, the lines of his face deep with sorrow. "But he has given us a sign. White Fawn must die to bring rain and save the tribe."

Little Bow stood motionless as Katakomo led White Fawn to a place at the edge of the village. Here a new lodge would be fashioned quickly, and here White Fawn would remain for two days,

unbound and unattended. For two days the sound of the drums would never stop. The braves would dance by turns, leaping, cupping their hands as if to catch rain, showing their faith that rain would come.

Little Bow could be brave no longer. He ran from the lodges along the dry stream and flung himself against his pony. He cried, with his face buried in Star's shaggy long mane.

The pony whinnied and nuzzled Little Bow's dark head. With his arms about Star's neck, Little Bow tried to think. There must be some other way to make rain. How could Katakomo know that the leaping of flames was a sign? How could he know the sign meant death to White Fawn?

If only I were older and wise and knew what to do, Little Bow thought. If Silver Arrow were here, he would know. He would never let White Fawn die.

Little Bow's heart beat faster. It was perhaps two days by horseback to the mountain, less time if one rode both day and night. He must take his pony and go to Silver Arrow.

Little Bow returned to the village and waited until dark. Then he slipped away to where Star was waiting under the cedar trees.

"You must find strength, my pretty pony," he said as he climbed onto Star's back. "We have a long journey ahead."

The pony tossed her head and began trotting along the stream bed with Little Bow on her back. The boy had never traveled at night. But he could not wait until daylight if he hoped to find Silver Arrow in time to save White Fawn.

He leaned along Star's neck and stroked her shaggy mane. "I trust you to follow the stream bed," he told her. "It will take us to the mountain."

Star trotted for a time, then picked her way through a winding canyon. Once she stumbled upon the rocks and Little Bow thought anxiously, what would happen if she sprained her leg so far from home? He made a prayer song to the Great Spirit to guide the pony safely.

When morning came, he saw that they were in rolling hills that stepped upward to the mountain. He must go carefully. When he had to cross a hill, he lifted his head only a little to see what might be beyond. Enemy tribes could be hunting anyplace, his father had often told him.

And recently a new danger had appeared. White men had come and made homes in a valley beyond the mountain.

Little Bow had never seen a white man but he had heard of them from Silver Arrow, who often guided the white missionary padres on long travels and could understand their language.

As the hot sun moved across the sky, Little Bow pressed his stomach close to his pony's back to still its hunger cries. Star was climbing each foothill slowly now. Little Bow scanned the hills for a sign of grass, but the land was as parched here as it was at home.

He patted Star's neck and encouraged her. "There will be cool water springs in the mountain and green grass around them."

Little Bow traveled on and came to a mound of sand in the stream bed. He knew a coyote had been digging there for water.

He jumped from his pony and ran and began to dig the hole deeper with his hands. Coyote was smart. All the other animals followed where he dug.

On his knees, Little Bow brought up a handful of damp sand. With both hands, he began to throw out sand between his legs, the way coyote would do.

Water trickled through his fingers. He cupped his hands, brought up muddy yellow liquid and began to drink, then turned to Star and held his hands to her nose.

She sucked up the water and moved in a little circle around him, whinnying as he dug for more.

Refreshed, they began to climb the steeper mountainside.

Night came quickly, as Silver Arrow had told him it did in the mountains. Little Bow looked about him. He had not planned how he would find Silver Arrow when he reached this place. He could see nothing but the trees overhead and the rocks in front of him.

Suddenly Star pricked up her ears. She began to trot, somehow finding new strength. Little Bow trusted her. He knew her nose and ears were keener than his. Perhaps she had discovered Silver Arrow's camp.

"Do you hear other horses?" he asked hopefully.

Star rounded a rock, hurried along a narrow canyon rim, slid down a slope so steep she had to throw her weight backward, almost sitting on her tail. She skidded to a halt beside a small mountain stream.

Little Bow slipped off her back and they drank the cool water side by side. He heard the pony breathing hard; she sucked in the water as if she had never had a drink before.

He pulled her away. She must not drink too much at once and be sick. He must let her rest for a while and eat grass and grow stronger.

He pulled a handful of leaves and began to rub her down, feeling the lean muscles under her black hide.

"E-ya, Star-in-the-face," he said, "you have done well this long night and day."

With a large tree branch by his side, he lay on his back and listened to Star cropping grass, filling her empty stomach. He knew he must be hungry too, but he could no longer feel it.

His mind was full of his sister. Only this night and tomorrow remained. Tomorrow night the rain dance would end. White Fawn would die if rain had not come. And he had not even found Silver Arrow yet!

He sat up, wondered if he dared push Star on now, but lay back again. His pony must rest or neither of them could go on.

He tried to fill his mind with good thoughts. There had been happy times in his village before the drought. He dozed off trying to remember those times.

When his eyes opened, he saw a light upon the mountain above him. He sat up, shaking. How long had he slept? Was the sun coming up? Then it would be too late to get back to the village and save his sister.

But it was not the sun. Flames leaped into the darkness a little way beyond him. Could it be the campfire of Silver Arrow? Little Bow scrambled to his feet and whistled for Star.

She trotted up to him and tossed her head. He leaped upon her back and pressed his knees against her sides to guide her toward the light.

He came to the edge of the trees and saw a wide flat ledge near the top of the mountain. Bonfires blazed in a semicircle behind a strange high pole. Across the pole, a little below the top, was fastened another, shorter one which looked like golden arms stretched out on each side.

Little Bow slid from his pony and watched quietly as three men in black robes moved forward. They stood before the crossed poles and began to chant in a strange language. These must be the white missionary padres. Then Silver Arrow should be here too. Little Bow started forward, then hid behind a tree.

He realized that these were prayer songs the padres sang around the fire. Perhaps they too were praying for rain and for a sign. He dared not approach them and ask for Silver Arrow.

Little Bow heard the padres sing the same words again and again:

> "He is risen, He is risen,
> This glorious Easter morn,
> He is risen!"

He could not understand what the strange words meant, but he felt the joy in the padres' voices. They must pray to a great God. They must love their God very much to sing with such happiness.

Star whinnied and tossed her head. Little Bow clapped his hand over her nose, and led her back among the trees. He was tying her to a tree branch when he heard footsteps behind him. A strong hand clasped his elbow and pinned him against the tree.

A patch of moonlight fell across Little Bow's face and a voice cried, "E-ya, Little Bow, you!"

Fear went out of Little Bow as he recognized Silver Arrow. Quickly he told his story of the searing heat which had come since Silver Arrow left the village. He told of the weeks without rain, of what had happened at the council fire, and of his sister's danger.

"When darkness comes again, White Fawn must die to please the Great Spirit and bring rain," he ended.

Silver Arrow stood as if he could not believe that he had heard right. Then he turned and ran to get his fastest horse. There was no time to lose if they hoped to reach the village before the next nightfall. Little Bow jumped onto Star.

"Hurry," Silver Arrow called as he rode up on his pony.

It was all Little Bow could do to keep up with Silver Arrow's swift flight down the mountainside. In the gray light before morning, he leaned forward on Star's neck, coaxing her to speed. The pony pricked up her ears as if she understood the great need for hurry.

When the sun rose, they stopped on the parched prairie and rubbed their horses down with the palms of their hands. Silver Arrow had brought a skin bag filled with water. They held water in their cupped hands for the ponies to drink.

"I saw the crossed trees on the mountain and heard the prayer chant of the black-robed padres," Little Bow said. "It was a great sign. I could feel it inside me. Is their God greater than our God? Is His medicine greater than that of the Great Spirit?"

"Their God and our God are the same God," Silver Arrow answered. "We only call Him different names, I think. But the white tribes have learned more about the Great Spirit than we know. They have much to teach us."

"Were the white padres singing new rain songs?" Little Bow asked. "What did they mean—'He is risen! He is risen!'"

"The padres were singing the ceremony of Easter," Silver Arrow said.

"Easter?" Little Bow asked. "What is Easter?"

Silver Arrow leaped on his horse. "I will tell you later of the mystery of Easter. Now we must hurry."

As they rode on and on, the blazing sun traveled across the sky and sank into the west. Little Bow's mind became frozen with fear. They would never reach the village in time to save his sister.

Dusk fell. They rode side by side now through the darkness. Neither pony could run anymore. They plodded with their heads down.

Finally they reached the last rise before the village. Little Bow heard the drums and singing. The braves were chanting the last prayer song of the rain dance.

Silver Arrow jumped from his horse and ran in long leaps ahead, leaving Little Bow behind. Little Bow knew he was too tired to keep up. He would follow with the horses.

Little Bow reached the top of the rise and looked down on the village below. The council circle was lighted by fires. White Fawn stood in the center of the circle. All the air seemed filled with a great emptiness as he saw the braves dancing nearer and nearer to her.

24

Suddenly a fierce cry rose above the songs of the people. The dancers fell back as if a spirit had appeared among them. Silver Arrow ran past the braves and placed himself in front of White Fawn.

When Little Bow reached the circle, he found that Silver Arrow was face to face with Katakomo, the only one who dared go forward.

"You have offended the Great Spirit," Katakomo cried, his face stricken with fear and concern for his tribe. "Now rain will never come and we shall all die."

"Hear me," Silver Arrow called, raising his right hand high. "You know Silver Arrow. Am I not always a speaker of truth?"

"E-ya," someone braver than the others called.

"E-ya, e-ya," the people chorused. They were not so afraid now. This was Silver Arrow, best singer of the tribe, mighty hunter, strong and graceful dancer. His word could be trusted. How could Silver Arrow displease the Great Spirit?

"I learned new things about the Great Spirit," Silver Arrow said, "from the white tribes from across the waters. Our people have always known the Great Spirit was good. But the white padres tell a tale, a true tale, of a great mystery that happened long ago—a mystery that changed the ways of all people."

"E-ya! E-ya!" the people cried.

Even Katakomo hesitated now, thinking that Silver Arrow might have learned a strange new mystery from the white padres. And it might be safer to respect a strange god until he learned how strong the god was. The medicine man sat down on the ground. The braves sat down, and all the people. They grew quiet.

Silver Arrow began to speak. "You know," he said, "I have been with the white missionary padres for three moons. I listened each night at their council fire. They know a strong mystery. I was a stranger but they did not try to hide their great medicine from me.

"The padres came here to tell it, they say. The Great Spirit wants them to tell everyone about His Son. He wants the men of every tribe and color to know His story."

Silver Arrow paused. He was about to speak words which

could not be said lightly.

"The great God loved all people so much, they say, that he sent His only Son to be born into the world. His Son lived and walked on the earth and taught men how to live. Then His Son died upon a cross. And anyone who believes in Him shall live again."

For a moment Little Bow sat among the people in silence, absorbing Silver Arrow's words, trying to understand their meaning.

"The Son was called Je-su," Silver Arrow went on. "When He died, He lay three days in death. Then the great God sent angels to roll away the rock before His Son's burial cave. The Son woke from death and walked forth—and from that day, all men knew that death is but a sleep."

Katakomo cried, "What has this tale to do with us? Our lungs are squeezed dry with hot air. Our throats are closed with dust. Only rain can save us. Remember the sign. White Fawn must die to please the Great Spirit."

Uneasily the people stirred. But Silver Arrow spoke quickly before they could move.

"If the great God loved people so much that He gave His Son to save them, He would not ask anyone to die to bring rain."

Little Bow saw that this was something to consider. The people nodded at the wisdom of this.

"The great God is pleased by *good lives*, not death," Silver Arrow said.

In the quiet and the firelight, the people looked at one another. They must decide. Little Bow knew that the chief had power, the medicine man had power, the council of braves had power, but the *last* power was in the vote of the people. It had always been so in his tribe.

Silver Arrow spoke again, slowly.

"This mystery of Easter is hard to understand. You cannot take it all inside you at once. But wait, its truth will grow upon you. I know. I helped build the cross upon the mountain there. I heard the tale again and again.

"The padres say that Je-su woke from death on the first Easter. He rose as the spring flowers rise from the brown earth after

their long winter's sleep.

"They say, when we see the earth put on new green grass and flowers, we must remember that Je-su rose from the grave. Je-su rose to teach us that our souls do not die. The real part of us is reborn, and lives forever.

"Think about this story. The Great Spirit will make the truth grow in you. Then you will know such joy and peace as you have never known."

Something in Silver Arrow's voice made Little Bow choke. His heart was moved as it had never been moved. He felt the same hush come upon all the people.

"Let White Fawn go," Silver Arrow said. "The Great Spirit

27

does not want us to take her life. He does not want us to take any life, the padres say."

"E-ya, e-ya," the people chorused.

Little Bow saw that the people believed Silver Arrow. They wanted his sister to live. He was so thankful that he felt too weak to move.

Over the heads of the people, Little Bow saw his sister smile at him. He knew she wanted to thank him for bringing Silver Arrow home, but she must also listen to the people. He tried to smile back at her but found he could not.

Little Bow turned to hide the tears quickly forming in his eyes, and so was the first to see the flash of light across the sky. He stood up, trembling, afraid to hope that what he saw was real.

The lightning zigged again between him and the mountain. It was followed by a low rumble.

The people heard the thunder too. They turned and saw another shimmer of light across the dark sky.

No one moved. Then all in the council ring broke into a wild dance of joy.

Drums beat the rain prayer. Figures leaped in the firelight and called out prayer songs of thankfulness.

Thunder and lightning seemed to dance with them as drops of rain began to fall. The people leaped and let the cool water fall upon their faces. They opened their mouths and drank it in.

Little Bow could hear the sound of water gushing over the dry stream bed. The torrent of rain put out the fires.

"Come, rain! We will build new fires," the people sang, and went on dancing in the dark.

Little Bow heard the happy, thankful people. He looked at the sky and saw lightning zigzag over his head. His heart made prayer songs so fast he could not say the words aloud. His sister was safe. The drought was ended. Silver Arrow was home and had told them of a great mystery.

Little Bow knew he would never forget this night. He was sure his people would always celebrate Easter with song and with fires, for they had learned of Easter around the fires of the rain dance.

Easter Morning

Aileen L. Fisher

We went out on an Easter morning,
Under the trees and the wide blue sky,
Up to the hill where the buds were swelling—
Mother and Father and Puck and I.

And I had hopes that we'd see a rabbit,
A brown little one with a cotton tail,
So we looked in the woods and under the bushes,
And followed what seemed like a rabbit trail.

We peeked and poked. But there wasn't a rabbit
Wherever we'd look or wherever we'd go,
Until I remembered, and said, "No wonder—
Easter's their busiest day, you know!"

The Velveteen Rabbit
by *Margery Williams*

There was once a velveteen rabbit, and in the beginning he was really splendid. He was fat and bunchy, as a rabbit should be; his coat was spotted brown and white, he had real thread whiskers, and his ears were lined with pink sateen. On Christmas morning, when he sat wedged in the top of the Boy's stocking with a sprig of holly between his paws, the effect was charming.

There were other things in the stocking, nuts and oranges and a toy engine, and chocolate almonds and a clockwork mouse, but the rabbit was quite the best of all. For at least two hours the Boy loved him, and then aunts and uncles came to dinner, and there was a great rustling of tissue paper and unwrapping of parcels, and in the excitement of looking at all the new presents the Velveteen Rabbit was forgotten.

For a long time he lived in the toy cupboard or on the nursery floor, and no one thought very much about him. As he was naturally shy, and only made of velveteen, some of the more expensive toys quite snubbed him. The mechanical toys were very superior, and looked down upon everyone else; they were full of modern ideas, and pretended they were real. The model boat, who had lived through two seasons and had lost most of his paint, caught the tone from them and never missed an opportunity of referring to his rigging in technical terms. The Rabbit could not claim to be a model of anything, for he didn't know that real rabbits existed; he thought they were all stuffed with sawdust like himself, and he understood that sawdust was quite out-of-date and should never be mentioned in modern circles. Even Timothy, the jointed wooden lion who was made by the disabled soldiers and should have had broader views, put on airs and pretended he was connected with Government. Between them all the poor little Rabbit was made to feel very insignificant and commonplace, and the only person who was kind to him at all was the Skin Horse.

The Skin Horse had lived longer in the nursery than any of the others. He was so old that his brown coat was bald in patches and showed the seams underneath, and most of the hairs in his tail had been pulled out to string bead necklaces. He was wise, for he had seen a long succession of mechanical toys arrive to boast and swagger, and by and by break their mainsprings and pass away, and he knew that they were only toys, and would never turn into anything else. For nursery magic is very strange and wonderful, and only those playthings that are old and wise and experienced like the Skin Horse understand all about it.

"What is REAL?" asked the Rabbit one day when they were lying side by side near the nursery fender, before Nana came to tidy the room. "Does it mean having things that buzz inside you and a stick-out handle?"

"Real isn't how you are made," said the Skin Horse. "It's a thing that happens to you. When a child loves you for a long, long time, not just to play with, but REALLY loves you, then you become Real."

"Does it hurt?" asked the Rabbit.

"Sometimes," said the Skin Horse, for he was always truthful. "When you are Real you don't mind being hurt."

"Does it happen all at once, like being wound up," he asked, "or bit by bit?"

"It doesn't happen all at once," said the Skin Horse. "You become. It takes a long time. That's why it doesn't often happen to people who break easily, or have sharp edges, or who have to be carefully kept. Generally, by the time you are Real, most of your hair has been loved off, and your eyes drop out and you get loose in the joints and very shabby. But these things don't matter at all, because once you are Real you can't be ugly, except to people who don't understand."

"I suppose *you* are Real?" said the Rabbit. And then he wished he had not said it, for he thought the Skin Horse might be sensitive. But the Skin Horse only smiled.

"The Boy's uncle made me Real," he said. "That was a great many years ago; but once you are Real you can't become unreal again. It lasts for always."

The Rabbit sighed. He thought it would be a long time before this magic called Real happened to him. He longed to become Real, to know what it felt like; and yet the idea of growing shabby and losing his eyes and whiskers was rather sad. He wished that he could become it without these uncomfortable things happening to him.

There was a person called Nana who ruled the nursery. Sometimes she took no notice of the playthings lying about, and sometimes, for no reason whatever, she went swooping about like a great wind and hustled them away in cupboards. She called this "tidying up," and the playthings all hated it, especially the tin ones. The Rabbit didn't mind it so much, for wherever he was thrown he came down soft.

One evening, when the Boy was going to bed, he couldn't find the china dog that always slept with him. Nana was in a hurry, and it was too much trouble to hunt for china dogs at bedtime, so she simply looked about her, and seeing that the toy cupboard door stood open, she made a swoop.

"Here," she said, "take your old Bunny! He'll do to sleep with you!" And she dragged the Rabbit out by one ear and put him into the Boy's arms.

That night, and for many nights after, the Velveteen Rabbit slept in the Boy's bed. At first he found it rather uncomfortable, for the Boy hugged him very tight, and sometimes he rolled over on him, and sometimes he pushed him so far under the pillow that the Rabbit could scarcely breathe. And he missed, too, those long moonlight hours in the nursery when all the house was silent, and his talks with the Skin Horse. But very soon he grew to like it, for the Boy would talk to him, and make nice tunnels for him under the bedclothes that he said were like the burrows the real rabbits lived in. And they had splendid games together, in whispers, when Nana went away to her supper and left the night-light burning on the mantelpiece. And when the Boy dropped off to sleep, the Rabbit would snuggle down close under his little warm chin and dream, with the Boy's hands clasped close round him all night long.

And so time went on, and the little Rabbit was very happy—so happy that he never noticed how his beautiful velveteen fur was getting shabbier and shabbier, and his tail coming unsewn, and all the pink rubbed off his nose where the Boy had kissed him.

Spring came, and they had long days in the garden, for wherever the Boy went the Rabbit went too. He had rides in the wheelbarrow, and picnics on the grass, and lovely fairy huts built for him under the raspberry canes behind the flower border. And once, when the Boy was called away suddenly to go out to tea, the Rabbit was left out on the lawn until long after dusk, and Nana had to come and look for him with the candle because the Boy couldn't go to sleep unless he was there. He was wet through with the dew and quite earthy from diving into the burrows the Boy had made for him in the flower bed, and Nana grumbled as she rubbed him off with a corner of her apron.

"You must have your old Bunny!" she said. "Fancy all that fuss for a toy!"

The Boy sat up in bed and stretched out his hands.

"Give me my Bunny!" he said. "You mustn't say that. He isn't a toy. He's REAL!"

When the little Rabbit heard that he was happy, for he knew that what the Skin Horse had said was true at last. The nursery magic had happened to him, and he was a toy no longer. He was Real. The Boy himself had said it.

That night he was almost too happy to sleep, and so much love stirred in his little sawdust heart that it almost burst. And into his boot-button eyes, which had long ago lost their polish, there came a look of wisdom and beauty, so that even Nana noticed it next morning when she picked him up, and said, "I declare if that old Bunny hasn't got quite a knowing expression!"

That was a wonderful summer!

Near the house where they lived there was a wood, and in the long June evenings the Boy liked to go there after tea to play. He took the Velveteen Rabbit with him, and before he wandered off to pick flowers, or play at brigands among the trees, he always made the Rabbit a little nest somewhere among the bracken where he would be quite cozy, for he was a kind-hearted little boy and he liked Bunny to be comfortable. One evening while the Rabbit was lying there alone, watching the ants that ran to and fro between his velvet paws in the grass, he saw two strange beings creep out of the tall bracken near him.

They were rabbits like himself, but quite furry and brand-new. They must have been very well made, for their seams didn't show at all, and they changed shape in a queer way when they moved; one minute they were long and thin and the next minute fat and bunchy, instead of always staying the same as he did. Their feet padded softly on the ground, and they crept quite close to him, twitching their noses, while the Rabbit stared hard to see which side the clockwork stuck out, for he knew that people who jump generally have something to wind them up. But he couldn't see it. They were evidently a new kind of rabbit altogether.

They stared at him, and the little Rabbit stared back. And all the time their noses twitched.

"Why don't you get up and play with us?" one of them asked.

"I don't feel like it," said the Rabbit, for he didn't want to explain that he had no clockwork.

"Ho!" said the furry rabbit. "It's as easy as anything!" And he gave a big hop sideways and stood on his hind legs.

"I don't believe you can!" he said.

"I can!" said the little Rabbit. "I can jump higher than anything!" He meant when the Boy threw him, but of course he didn't want to say so.

"Can you hop on your hind legs?" asked the furry rabbit.

That was a dreadful question, for the Velveteen Rabbit had no

38

hind legs at all! The back of him was made all in one piece, like a pincushion. He sat still in the bracken, and hoped that the other rabbits wouldn't notice. "I don't want to!" he said again.

But the wild rabbits have very sharp eyes. And this one stretched out his neck and looked.

"He hasn't got any hind legs!" he called out. "Fancy a rabbit without any hind legs!" And he began to laugh.

"I have!" cried the little Rabbit. "I have got hind legs! I am sitting on them!"

"Then stretch them out and show me, like this!" said the wild rabbit. And he began to whirl round and dance, till the little Rabbit got quite dizzy.

"I don't like dancing," he said. "I'd rather sit still!"

But all the while he was longing to dance, for a funny new tickly feeling ran through him, and he felt he would give anything in the world to be able to jump about as these rabbits did.

The strange rabbit stopped dancing, and came quite close. He came so close this time that his long whiskers brushed the Velveteen Rabbit's ear, and then he wrinkled his nose suddenly and flattened his ears and jumped backwards.

"He doesn't smell right!" he exclaimed. "He isn't a rabbit at all! He isn't real!"

"I *am* Real!" said the little Rabbit. "I am Real! The Boy said so!" And he nearly began to cry.

Just then there was a sound of footsteps, and the Boy ran past near them, and with a stamp of feet and a flash of white tails the two strange rabbits disappeared.

"Come back and play with me!" called the little Rabbit. "Oh, do come back! I *know* I am Real!"

But there was no answer, only the little ants ran to and fro, and the bracken swayed gently where the two strangers had passed. The Velveteen Rabbit was all alone.

"Oh dear!" he thought. "Why did they run away like that? Why couldn't they stop and talk to me?"

For a long time he lay very still, watching the bracken and hoping that they would come back. But they never returned, and presently the sun sank lower and the little white moths fluttered out, and the Boy came and carried him home.

Weeks passed, and the little Rabbit grew very old and shabby, but the Boy loved him just as much. He loved him so hard that he loved all his whiskers off, and the pink lining to his ears turned gray, and his brown spots faded. He even began to lose his shape, and he scarcely looked like a rabbit anymore, except to the Boy. To him he was always beautiful, and that was all that the little Rabbit cared about. He didn't mind how he looked to other people, because the nursery magic had made him Real, and when you are Real shabbiness doesn't matter.

And then, one day, the Boy was ill.

His face grew very flushed, and he talked in his sleep, and his little body was so hot that it burned the Rabbit when he held him close. Strange people came and went in the nursery, and a light burned all night, and through it all the little Velveteen Rabbit lay there, hidden from sight under the bedclothes, and he never stirred, for he was afraid that if they found him someone might take him away, and he knew that the Boy needed him.

It was a long, weary time, for the Boy was too ill to play, and the little Rabbit found it rather dull with nothing to do all day long. But he snuggled down patiently, and looked forward to the time when the Boy should be well again and they would go out in the garden amongst the flowers and the butterflies and play splendid games in the raspberry thicket as they used to. All sorts of delightful things he planned, and while the Boy lay half asleep he crept up close to the pillow and whispered them in his ear. And presently the fever turned, and the Boy got better. He was able to sit up in bed and look at picture books, while the little Rabbit cuddled close at his side. And one day, they let him get up and dress.

It was a bright, sunny morning, and the windows stood wide open. They had carried the Boy out onto the balcony, wrapped in a shawl, and the little Rabbit lay tangled up among the bedclothes, thinking. The Boy was going to the seaside tomorrow. Everything was arranged, and now it only remained to carry out the doctor's orders. They talked about it all, while the little Rabbit lay under the bedclothes, with just his head peeping out, and listened. The room was to be disinfected, and all the books and toys that the Boy had played with in bed must be burnt.

"Hurrah!" thought the little Rabbit. "Tomorrow we shall go to the seaside!" For the Boy had often talked of the seaside, and he wanted very much to see the big waves coming in, and the tiny crabs, and the sand castles.

Just then Nana caught sight of him.

"How about his old Bunny?" she asked.

"*That?*" said the doctor. "Why, it's a mass of scarlet fever germs!—Burn it at once. What? Nonsense! Get him a new one. He mustn't have that anymore!"

And so the little Rabbit was put into a sack with the old picture books and a lot of rubbish, and carried out to the end of the garden behind the fowl house. That was a fine place to make a bonfire, only the gardener was too busy just then to attend to it. He had the potatoes to dig and the green peas to gather, but next morning he promised to come quite early and burn the whole lot.

That night the Boy slept in a different bedroom, and he had a new bunny to sleep with him. It was a splendid bunny, all white plush with real glass eyes, but the Boy was too excited to care very much about it. For tomorrow he was going to the seaside, and that in itself was such a wonderful thing that he could think of nothing else.

And while the Boy was asleep, dreaming of the seaside, the little Rabbit lay among the old picture books in the corner behind the fowl house, and he felt very lonely. The sack had been left untied, and so by wriggling a bit he was able to get his head through the opening and look out. He was shivering a little, for he had always been used to sleeping in a proper bed, and by this time his coat had worn so thin and threadbare from hugging that it was no longer any protection to him. Nearby he could see the thicket of raspberry canes, growing tall and close like a tropical jungle, in whose shadow he had played with the Boy on bygone mornings. He thought of those long, sunlit hours in the garden— how happy they were!—and a great sadness came over him. He seemed to see them all pass before him, each more beautiful than the other, the fairy huts in the flower bed, the quiet evenings in the wood when he lay in the bracken and the little ants ran over his paws; the wonderful day when he first knew that he was Real. He thought of the Skin Horse, so wise and gentle, and all that he had told him. Of what use was it to be loved and lose one's beauty and become Real if it all ended like this? And a tear, a real tear, trickled down his little shabby velvet nose and fell to the ground.

And then a strange thing happened. For where the tear had fallen a flower grew out of the ground, a mysterious flower, not at all like any that grew in the garden. It had slender green leaves the color of emeralds, and in the center of the leaves a blossom like a golden cup. It was so beautiful that the little Rabbit forgot to cry, and just lay there watching it. And presently the blossom

opened, and out of it there stepped a fairy.

She was quite the loveliest fairy in the whole world. Her dress was of pearl and dewdrops, and there were flowers round her neck and in her hair, and her face was like the most perfect flower of all. And she came close to the little Rabbit and gathered him up in her arms and kissed him on his velveteen nose that was all damp from crying.

"Little Rabbit," she said, "don't you know who I am?"

The Rabbit looked up at her, and it seemed to him that he had seen her face before, but he couldn't think where.

"I am the nursery magic Fairy," she said. "I take care of all the playthings that the children have loved. When they are old and worn out and the children don't need them anymore, then I come and take them away with me and turn them into Real."

"Wasn't I Real before?" asked the little Rabbit.

"You were Real to the Boy," the Fairy said, "because he loved you. Now you shall be Real to everyone."

And she held the little Rabbit close in her arms and flew with him into the wood.

It was light now, for the moon had risen. All the forest was beautiful, and the fronds of the bracken shone like frosted silver. In the open glade between the tree trunks the wild rabbits danced with their shadows on the velvet grass, but when they saw the Fairy they all stopped dancing and stood round in a ring to stare at her.

"I've brought you a new playfellow," the Fairy said. "You must be very kind to him and teach him all he needs to know in Rabbit Land, for he is going to live with you for ever and ever!"

And she kissed the little Rabbit again and put him down on the grass.

"Run and play, little Rabbit!" she said.

But the little Rabbit sat quite still for a moment and never moved. For when he saw all the wild rabbits dancing around him he suddenly remembered about his hind legs, and he didn't want them to see that he was made all in one piece. He did not know that when the Fairy kissed him that last time she had changed him altogether. And he might have sat there a long time, too shy to move, if just then something hadn't tickled his nose, and before he thought what he was doing he lifted his hind toe to scratch it.

And he found that he actually had hind legs! Instead of dingy velveteen, he had brown fur, soft and shiny, his ears twitched by themselves, and his whiskers were so long that they brushed the grass. He gave one leap, and the joy of using those hind legs was so great that he went springing about the turf on them, jumping sideways and whirling round as the others did, and he grew so excited that when at last he did stop to look for the Fairy she had gone.

He was a Real Rabbit at last, at home with the other rabbits. Autumn passed and winter, and in the spring, when the days grew warm and sunny, the Boy went out to play in the wood behind the house. And while he was playing, two rabbits crept out from the bracken and peeped at him. One of them was brown all over, but the other had strange markings under his fur, as though long ago he had been spotted, and the spots still showed through. And about his little soft nose and his round black eyes there was something familiar, so that the Boy thought to himself:

"Why, he looks just like my old Bunny that was lost when I had scarlet fever!"

But he never knew that it really was his own Bunny, come back to look at the child who had first helped him to be Real.

Meeting
The Easter Bunny

Rowena Bennett

On Easter morn at early dawn
  before the cocks were crowing,
I met a bobtail bunnykin
  and asked where he was going.
" 'Tis in the house and out the house
  a-tipsy, tipsy-toeing,
'Tis round the house and 'bout the house
  a-lightly I am going."
"But what is that of every hue
  you carry in your basket?"
" 'Tis eggs of gold and eggs of blue;
  I wonder that you ask it.
'Tis chocolate eggs and bonbon eggs
  and eggs of red and gray,
For every child in every house
  on bonny Easter Day."
He perked his ears and winked his eye
  and twitched his little nose;
He shook his tail—what tail he had—
  and stood up on his toes.
"I must be gone before the sun;
  the East is growing gray;
'Tis almost time for bells to chime,"
  so he hippety-hopped away.

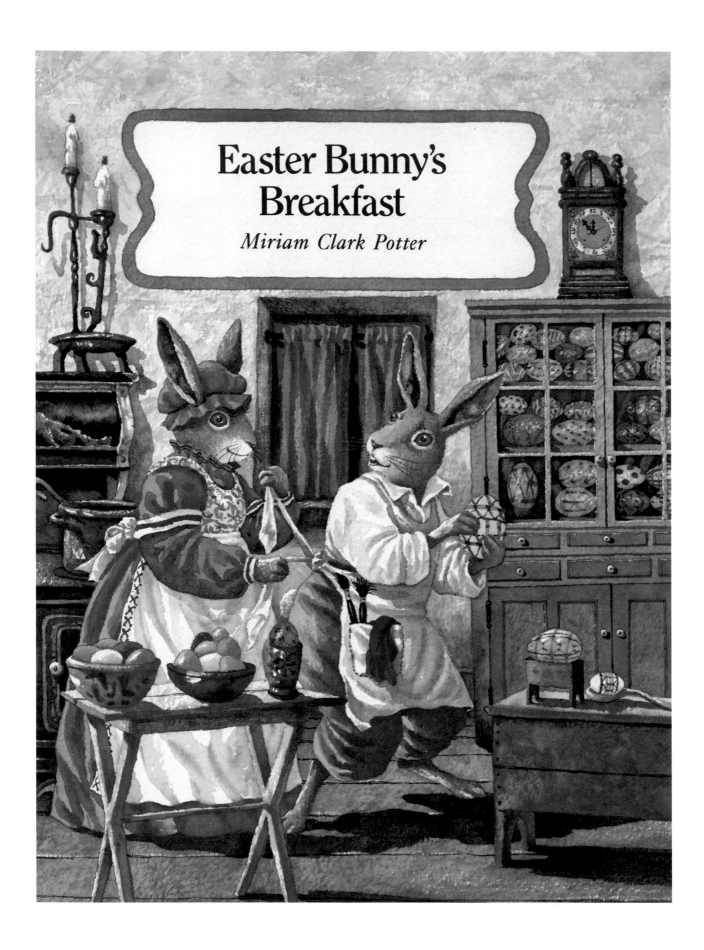

Easter Bunny's Breakfast

Miriam Clark Potter

Eggs, eggs, eggs were all around Easter Bunny's little house. For it was the night before Easter, and he was all ready to take them to the sleeping children.

Sugar eggs, chocolate eggs, hard-cooked eggs with flowers painted on their shells, marshmallow eggs and maple ones, all stood waiting to be packed into his basket. Easter Bunny had worked hard for a great many days to finish them.

"It's been a lot of work," said Mrs. Bunny as she untied his big blue apron. "But you do make such wonderful, good-to-eat eggs! Very specially good they are this year, too. Better than ever!"

"I don't think so," said Easter Bunny a little crossly. "I don't like them."

"That's because you've been shut up so long in the sugar-smelly kitchen," thought Mrs. Bunny to herself. Aloud she said, "Well, we'd better put them into the basket now. It's almost midnight by our little wooden clock. Time for you to start."

"All right." Easter Bunny gave a big sigh. "I'll put on my hat and coat—it's cold outdoors. Please have a good hot breakfast for me when I get back, won't you, my dear?"

"Why, of course," said Mrs. Bunny. "I'll have milk, and pancakes, and eggs. How shall I fix them?"

"Oh, no eggs!" said Easter Bunny. "I don't want any eggs! Why, I've seen just eggs and eggs for days and days!"

"All right," said Mrs. Bunny. "Just milk and pancakes."

"But no *eggs!*" said Easter Bunny, with a little shout.

"All right. Here's your basket. Good-bye, and I do hope you have good luck."

"I hope the children won't wake up," said Easter Bunny. "I have to be so quick, and so quiet, hiding all these eggs."

"You'll be all right," said Mrs. Bunny. "I'll be waiting for you."

"Good-bye," and Easter Bunny scuttled off into the dark woods. After a while he turned back and called something. He was so far away that Mrs. Bunny could hardly hear.

"What?" she called to him.

"NO—*eggs!*" shouted Easter Bunny, and then he was gone.

Mrs. Bunny smiled a bunny smile to herself, and then she

stood at the door a minute sniffing the cold air. "No spring smells yet," she said, and gave a little sigh. Then she thought of the sleeping children, and how happy they would be when they woke up in the morning with their Easter eggs. "Now I'll have a little nap, and then it will be time to get breakfast," she told her sleepy self. So she sat down in her favorite blue rocking chair and shut her eyes, and very soon nice sleepy feelings began to come over her. Her paws hung down softly and her nap had begun.

"One—two—three—four—" It was the little wooden clock striking. Mrs. Bunny woke up with a jump and a little scuttle. She dashed down her cellar stairs. Easter Bunny would be coming back soon and it was more than time to begin his breakfast.

"I must get the milk," said Mrs. Bunny, reaching up to her cellar shelf. She carried the little blue pail up and put it on the kitchen table. But, oh, how queer and thick the milk looked! "It's sour. He can't drink sour milk. Oh, dear! Well, it will be just right for the pancakes." And she rushed over to the little cupboard, where the flour was kept.

But what was this? Little bad scratchy toe tracks all around the flour can! "Those naughty little field mice," said Mrs. Bunny. "They've eaten up all my flour. I shall have to tell their mother—they really must learn to behave themselves. But what shall I give Easter Bunny for his breakfast? He said milk—and that is sour. He said pancakes—and the flour is all gobbled up. And he said *no eggs*. And all I have to eat in the house is eggs—six eggs—all fresh and delicious. What shall I do?"

Just then she heard a little crackling in the woods. "Goodness me, he's coming," she thought. And she popped the eggs into hot water to cook.

There was a little scratching at the door. Mrs. Bunny went to see. It wasn't Easter Bunny at all; it was Red Squirrel from the creaky oak tree. "How do you do, Mrs. Bunny," he said. "The pussy willows are out. I just thought you'd like to know."

"Why, how lovely!" Mrs. Bunny clapped her paws. "I'm so glad that's happened. Spring is really beginning."

"Yes," said the little squirrel, and off he ran.

Mrs. Bunny took a peek at the eggs. They were cooking nicely.

Then there was another scuttle at the door.

It was Little Chipmunk, from down by the frog pond. Mrs. Bunny had not seen him for a long time. "Hello, Mrs. Bunny," he squeaked. "The bluebirds have finished their nest. I was sure you'd like to hear about it."

"Why, of course I'd like to hear about it!" said Mrs. Bunny. "How good of you to scamper over here this very early morning to tell me about it. Good!" And off scampered Little Chipmunk.

Then Mrs. Bunny stuck her ears up, for she heard a little thin sound far away, a little cold sweet sound like wind music.

"The frogs are beginning to sing," she said to herself. "Oh, what lots of good news I shall have to tell Easter Bunny when he comes back! If I weren't so worried about his breakfast I should be so happy!"

Just then she *did* hear a scuttle. Yes, this time it was Easter Bunny; he came hopping through the woods with his hat in his paw. His empty bag hung over his back.

"Hello, my dear," he said. "I took the eggs around—lots of houses, many gardens; not a child woke up. Good luck, I call that!"

"Yes, good luck." Mrs. Bunny smiled. But to herself she thought, "Oh, dear; I must tell him about his eggs—for—breakfast."

But Easter Bunny went on talking happily.

"I've got the best news!" he said. "I met Red Squirrel, and he told me the pussy willows are out—"

"Yes," said Mrs. Bunny, "he was here too."

"And then along came Little Chipmunk."

"And he told you the bluebirds have finished their nest." Mrs. Bunny laughed. "He came to tell me—the good thing—"

"And I heard *frogs*," chattered Easter Bunny. "Well, is my breakfast ready?"

"All ready," said Mrs. Bunny, and she put the hot covered dish before him.

Easter Bunny lifted the cover off. "Why, *eggs!*" he said. "How good they look!"

Mrs. Bunny was so surprised that she nearly fell over the little blue rocking chair.

"I was going to get you pancakes and milk, too," she said, "but I had two disappointments. First, the milk was sour, and then I found that those bad little field mice had gobbled up all our flour. So all you have is eggs!"

Easter Bunny laughed. "Well, never mind," he said. "I feel so happy about the good luck I had—and the pussy willows coming

out—and the bluebirds and the frogs—that I don't mind at all. It's so nice to have spring beginning! Eggs are just the thing for Easter breakfast, after all, aren't they?"

"Yes," said Mrs. Bunny, "I guess they are. Happy Easter! Here comes the sun over the top of the hill."

And Easter Bunny began to crack open his eggs.

Baby Seed Song

Edith Nesbit

Little brown brother, oh! little brown brother,
   Are you awake in the dark?
Here we lie cozily, close to each other:
   Hark to the song of the lark—
"Waken!" the lark says, "waken and dress you;
   Put on your green coats and gay,
Blue sky will shine on you, sunshine caress you—
   Waken! 'tis morning—'tis May!"

Little brown brother, oh! little brown brother,
   What kind of flower will you be?
I'll be a poppy—all white, like my mother;
   Do be a poppy like me.
What! you're a sunflower? How I shall miss you
   When you're grown golden and high!
But I shall send all the bees up to kiss you;
   Little brown brother, good-bye.

The Selfish Giant
by Oscar Wilde

Every afternoon as they were coming from school, the children used to go and play in the Giant's garden.

It was a large, lovely garden with soft green grass. Here and there over the grass stood beautiful flowers like stars, and there were twelve peach trees that in the springtime broke out into delicate blossoms of pink and pearl, and in the autumn bore rich fruit.

The birds sat on the trees and sang so sweetly that the children used to stop their games to listen to them. "How happy we are here!" they cried to each other.

One day the Giant came back. He had been to visit his friend the Cornish ogre, and had stayed with him for seven years. After the seven years were over he had said all that he had to say, for his conversation was limited, and he determined to return to his own castle. When he arrived he saw the children playing in the garden.

"What are you doing here?" he cried in a very gruff voice, and the children ran away.

"My own garden is my own garden," said the Giant. "Anyone can understand that, and I will allow nobody to play in it but myself." So he built a high wall all around it, and put up a notice board:

TRESPASSERS WILL BE PROSECUTED

He was a very selfish giant.

The poor children had now nowhere to play. They tried to play on the road, but the road was very dusty and full of hard stones, and they did not like it. They used to wander round the high wall when their lessons were over, and talk about the beautiful garden inside. "How happy we were there," they said to each other.

Then the Spring came, and all over the country there were little blossoms and little birds. Only in the garden of the Selfish Giant it was still winter. The birds did not care to sing in it, as there were no children, and the trees forgot to blossom.

Once a beautiful flower put its head out from the grass, but when it saw the notice board it was so sorry for the children that it slipped back into the ground again, and went off to sleep. The only people who were pleased were the Snow and the Frost. "Spring has forgotten this garden," they cried, "so we will live here all the year round."

The Snow covered up the grass with her great white cloak, and the Frost painted all the trees silver. Then they invited the North Wind to stay with them, and he came. He was wrapped in furs, and he roared all day about the garden, and blew the chimney pots down. "This is a delightful spot," he said; "we must ask the Hail on a visit."

So the Hail came. Every day for three hours he rattled on the roof of the castle till he broke most of the slates, and then he ran round and round the garden as fast as he could go. He was dressed in gray, and his breath was like ice.

"I cannot understand why the Spring is so late in coming," said the Selfish Giant, as he sat at the window and looked out at his cold white garden; "I hope there will be a change in the weather."

But the Spring never came, nor the Summer. The Autumn gave golden fruit to every garden, but to the Giant's garden she gave none. "He is too selfish," she said. So it was always Winter there, and the North Wind, and the Hail, and the Frost, and the Snow danced about through the trees.

One morning the Giant was lying awake in bed when he heard some lovely music. It sounded so sweet to his ears that he thought it must be the King's musicians passing by. It was really only a little linnet singing outside his window, but it was so long since he had heard a bird sing in his garden that it seemed to him to be the most beautiful music in the world.

Then the Hail stopped dancing over his head, and the North Wind ceased roaring, and a delicious perfume came to him through the open casement. "I believe the Spring has come at last," said the Giant, and he jumped out of bed and looked out.

What did he see?

He saw a most wonderful sight. Through a little hole in the wall the children had crept in, and they were sitting in the branches of the trees. In every tree that he could see there was a

little child. And the trees were so glad to have the children back again that they had covered themselves with blossoms, and were waving their arms gently above the children's heads. The birds were flying about and twittering with delight, and the flowers were looking up through the green grass and laughing.

It was a lovely scene, only in one corner it was still Winter. It was the farthest corner of the garden, and in it was standing a little boy. He was so small that he could not reach up to the branches of the tree, and he was wandering all round it, crying bitterly. The poor tree was still quite covered with frost and snow, and the North Wind was blowing and roaring above it.

"Climb up! little boy," said the tree, and it bent its branches down as low as it could; but the boy was too tiny.

And the Giant's heart melted as he looked out. "How selfish I have been!" he said; "now I know why the Spring would not come here. I will put that poor little boy on the top of the tree, and then I will knock down the wall, and my garden shall be the children's playground for ever and ever." He was really very sorry for what he had done.

So he crept downstairs and opened the front door quite softly, and went out into the garden. But when the children saw him they were so frightened that they all ran away, and the garden became Winter again. Only the little boy did not run, for his eyes were so full of tears that he did not see the Giant coming. And the Giant strode up behind him and took him gently in his hand, and put him up into the tree.

The tree broke at once into blossom, and the birds came and sang on it, and the little boy stretched out his two arms and flung them around the Giant's neck and kissed him. And the other children, when they saw that the Giant was not wicked any longer, came running back; and with them came the Spring.

"It is your garden now, little children," said the Giant, and he took a great ax and knocked down the wall. And when the people were going to market at twelve o'clock they found the Giant playing with the children in the most beautiful garden they had ever seen.

All day long they played, and in the evening they came to the Giant to bid him good-bye.

"But where is your little companion," he said, "the boy I put into the tree?" The Giant loved him the best because he had kissed him.

"We don't know," answered the children. "He has gone away."

"You must tell him to be sure and come here tomorrow," said the Giant. But the children said that they did not know where he lived, and had never seen him before; and the Giant felt very sad.

Every afternoon when school was over, the children came and played with the Giant. But the little boy whom the Giant loved was never seen again. The Giant was very kind to all the children, yet he longed for his first little friend, and often spoke of

him. "How I would like to see him!" he used to say.

Years went by, and the Giant grew very old and feeble. He could not play about anymore, so he sat in a huge armchair and watched the children at their games, and admired his garden. "I have many beautiful flowers," he said, "but the children are the most beautiful flowers of all."

One winter morning he looked out of his window as he was dressing. He did not hate the Winter now, for he knew that it was merely Spring asleep, and that the flowers were resting.

Suddenly he rubbed his eyes in wonder, and looked and looked. It certainly was a marvelous sight. In the farthest corner of the garden was a tree quite covered with lovely white blossoms. Its branches were all golden, and silver fruit hung down from them, and underneath it stood the little boy he had loved.

Downstairs ran the Giant in great joy, and out into the garden. He hastened across, and came near to the child. And when he came quite close his face grew red with anger, and he said, "Who hath dared to wound thee?" For on the palms of the child's hands were the prints of two nails, and the prints of two nails on the little feet.

"Who hath dared to wound thee?" cried the Giant. "Tell me, that I may take my big sword and slay him."

"Nay!" answered the child; "but these are the wounds of Love."

"Who art thou?" said the Giant, and a strange awe fell on him, and he knelt before the little child.

And the child smiled on the Giant, and said to him, "You let me play once in your garden; today you shall come with me to my garden, which is Paradise."

And when the children ran in that afternoon, they found the Giant lying dead under the tree, all covered with white blossoms.